The PRINCE'S NEW PET

BRIAN ANDERSON

A NEAL PORTER BOOK · ROARING BROOK PRESS · NEW YORK

For Liam and Sophie, my prince and my pet

Copyright © 2011 by Brian Anderson
A Neal Porter Book
Published by Roaring Brook Press
Roaring Brook Press is a division of Holtzbrinck Publishing Holdings Limited Partnership
175 Fifth Avenue, New York, New York 10010
mackids.com

Library of Congress Cataloging-in-Publication Data

Anderson, Brian, 1974–
    The Prince's new pet / Brian Anderson. – 1st ed.
        p. cm.
    Summary: In a gray and colorless kingdom, the Prince receives an unusual
colorful new pet for his birthday.
    ISBN 978-1-59643-357-1
    [1. Princes—Fiction. 2. Color—Fiction. 3. Pets—Fiction.] I. Title.

    PZ7.A5228Pr 2011
    [E]—dc22

                                2010036798

Roaring Brook Press books are available for special promotions and premiums.
For details contact: Director of Special Markets, Holtzbrinck Publishers.

First edition 2011
Book design by Jennifer Browne
Printed in August 2011 in China by South China Printing Co. Ltd., Dongguan City, Guangdong Province

10 9 8 7 6 5 4 3 2 1

It was Prince Viridian's birthday.

"What a miserable day," he sighed, and watched as the smogafiers blotted out the sun and the royal painters sloshed the countryside with a fresh coat of gray paint.

The Prince's mother, Queen Perylene, had loved colors— she had even built factories that created new ones.

Although she died on his second birthday, the Prince remembered the vivid parade of colors that followed her everywhere.

To mourn her, King Cerulean had banned all color from the kingdom.

"You are very lucky, Mister Spider," said the Prince.
"You don't have to go to my birthday party. Best not
to keep everyone waiting. The sooner it starts
the sooner it will be over."

Prince Viridian plodded
through the Great Hall.
Large, empty frames filled
with cobwebs lined the walls. He
paused briefly at each frame, trying to
imagine the vibrant paintings that
once filled them.

In his despair the King had appointed
a royal color catcher to banish every
bit of color from the kingdom. He was
an ambitious man who was very good
at his job. Some might say too good.

The Prince stepped through
a doorway into the dreary
courtyard beyond.

He shuffled past the
Duchess of Humdrum,
the Archduke of Monotonous,
the Baroness of Blah, and
other members of the
royal court.

A stack of gifts wrapped in
gray paper, tied with gray
ribbons were piled next to
the gray birthday cake.

It was the same licorice-
flavored cake as last year and
the year before that: eight
layers of gray cake smeared
with gray frosting without
a single candle.

"Happy birthday, son,"
sighed King Cerulean as he
slumped in his throne.

His Royal Grayness waved to the royal waiters,
who silently sliced and distributed gray cake to all.

As the guests nibbled their cake in silence, a vast shadow slowly blanketed the courtyard.

Suddenly, the Baroness of Blah shrieked, as plates shattered on the floor.

The King bellowed,
"Remove it at once!"
The royal guards, armor
rattling, crept toward the
splintered chest.

And then something
wondrous sprang from it.

"Summon the royal color catcher!"
roared the King.

But no summons was needed. He
lurched after the wooglefoof,
waving a long net over
his head.

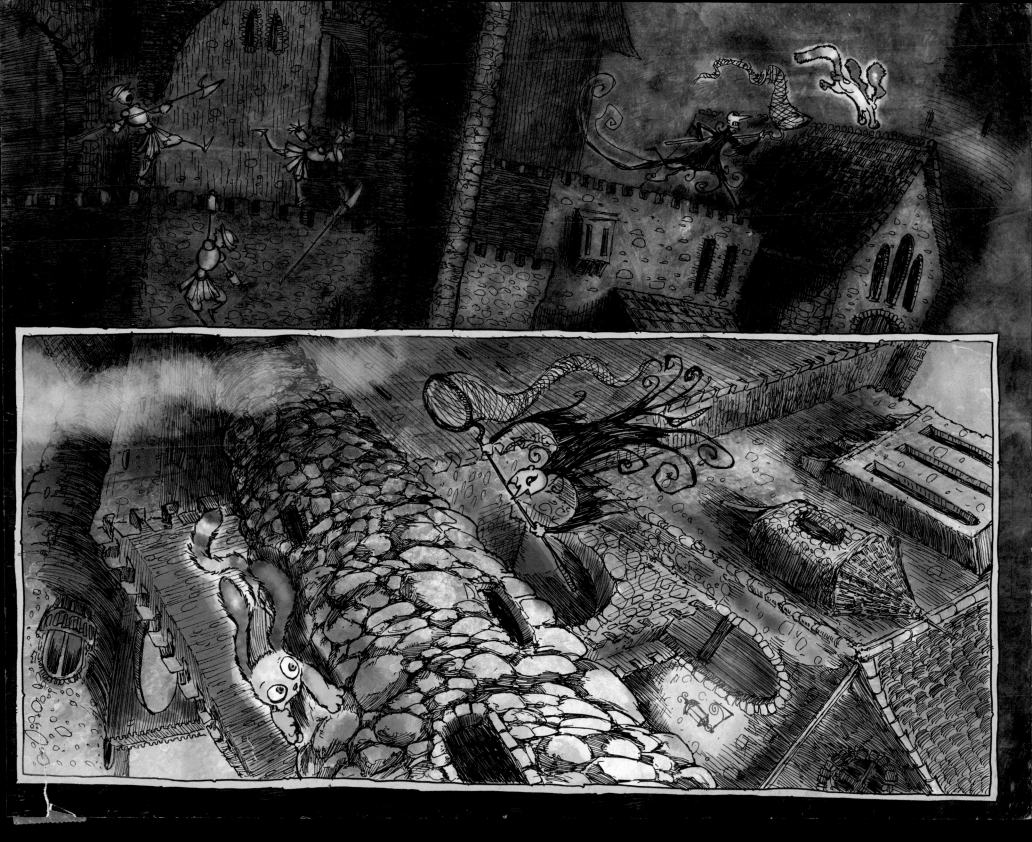

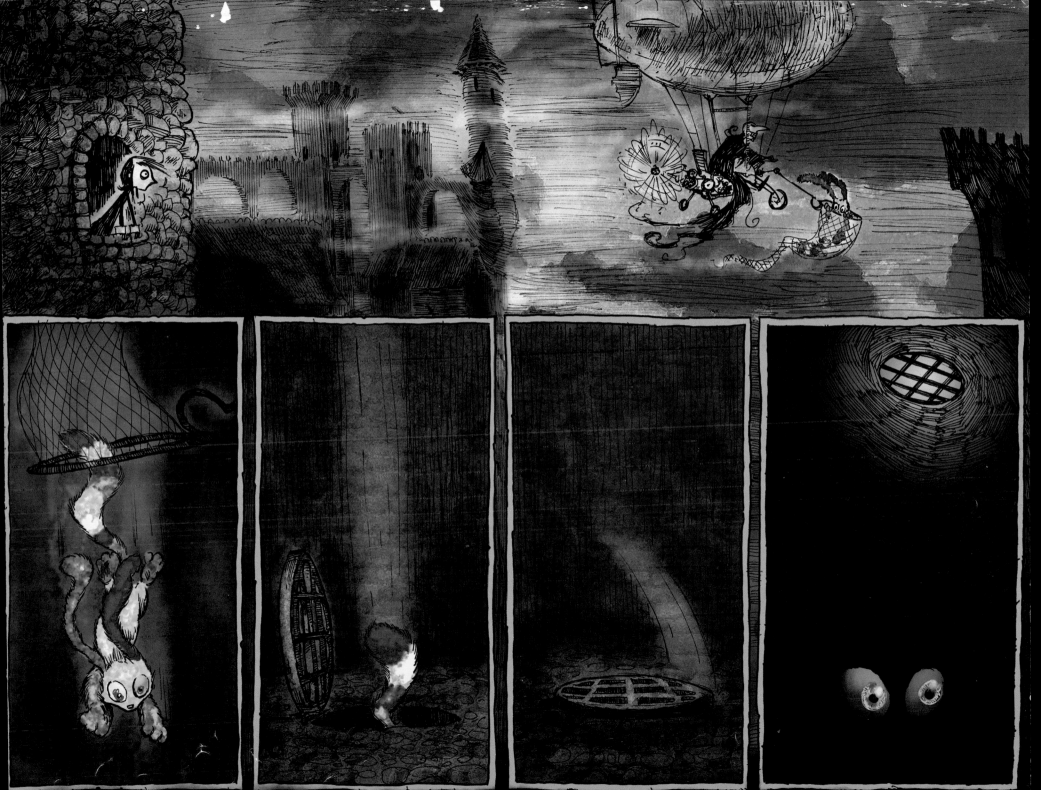

King Cerulean shuffled into the Prince's room.

"I'm sorry you could not keep your new pet, but rules are rules," he said with a sigh.

"They are stupid rules," said the Prince.

The King gently laid his hand on his son's shoulder. Prince Viridian jerked it away.

"Mom never would have allowed such stupid rules!"

"Your mother loved color," said the King, as he gazed out the window. "After she passed, every flower, every color reminded me of her. I couldn't bear it."

Cerulean turned away, wiping his
cheeks. "Maybe when you are King,
you can change the rules."

He left, stifling a sob.

"When I am King I *will* change
them!" said the Prince.

A shadow hovered outside the Prince's
doorway. The royal color catcher smirked,
revealing an impossible number of teeth.
"Oh, little Prince, then we must make
sure you never become King!" he hissed.

THUD!

The Prince collapsed on his bed, tears dampening his pillow.
Suddenly the spider dangled before his eyes, bouncing frantically
on the end of its thread. Prince Viridian noticed something clutched
in his pincers: a small tuft of brightly colored fur!
"You know where the wooglefoof is?" asked the Prince.

The spider dropped
to the ground,
scurrying across
the floor and
out the door.

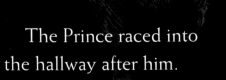

The Prince raced into
the hallway after him.

"My Lord. Murialis Mayhew, royal court painter, at your disposal."

"Are you going to eat us?" asked the Prince.

"Eat you? Good gracious gumballs, no! We shall have some tea, and then maybe you'll let me capture your likeness on a canvas."

Murialis stood straightening her tattered clothes.

"Come this way."

The royal painter skipped down the dank tunnel. The Prince and the wooglefoof followed . . . at a safe distance.

"Now where were we? Oh yes, trapped in the dungeon!
Heh heh . . . Sorry, just a little prison humor," said Murialis.
"Why are you here?" asked Prince Viridian.

"After I refused to repaint all the
royal paintings in black and
white, the royal color catcher
tossed me in here."

"I'm so sorry," said the Prince.

"No need to be sorry," said Murialis.
"I'm happy as a bee down here with all the colors!"
"It *is* nice to finally see some color,
but it's still a dungeon. We've got to get out of here.
Can you show us the way?" asked the Prince.

"Here we are," said Murialis. "Out and through that grate and you're free!"

Before the Prince could thank her, a shadowy figure loomed over them.

"Oh, I think the Prince and his peculiar friend will be staying for a while . . . Perhaps forever!" said the royal color catcher, as he slinked toward them.

"You!" cried Murialis.

The royal
color catcher
shoved the
painter into a
murky cell and flung
the iron door shut.

The Prince and the wooglefoof
raced off back into the darkness with
the royal color catcher in pursuit.

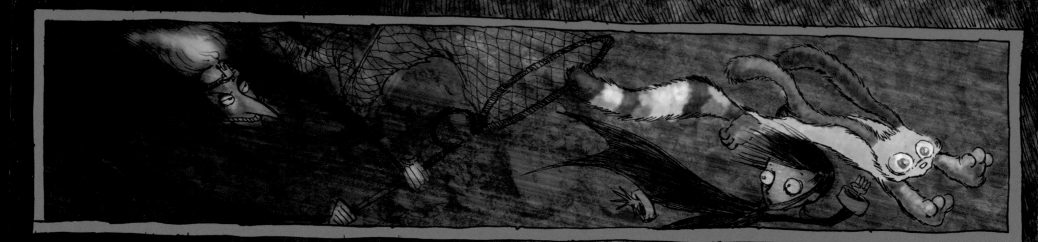

"I'll get you! And then your father! The whole kingdom will soon be mine!" shrieked the color catcher.

The wooglefoof skidded to a halt and grabbed the Prince, stopping him inches away from a cavernous abyss.
"Nowhere to run, my little friends?" cackled the color catcher.

"You could save me a bit of work and jump, my dear Prince," he hissed.

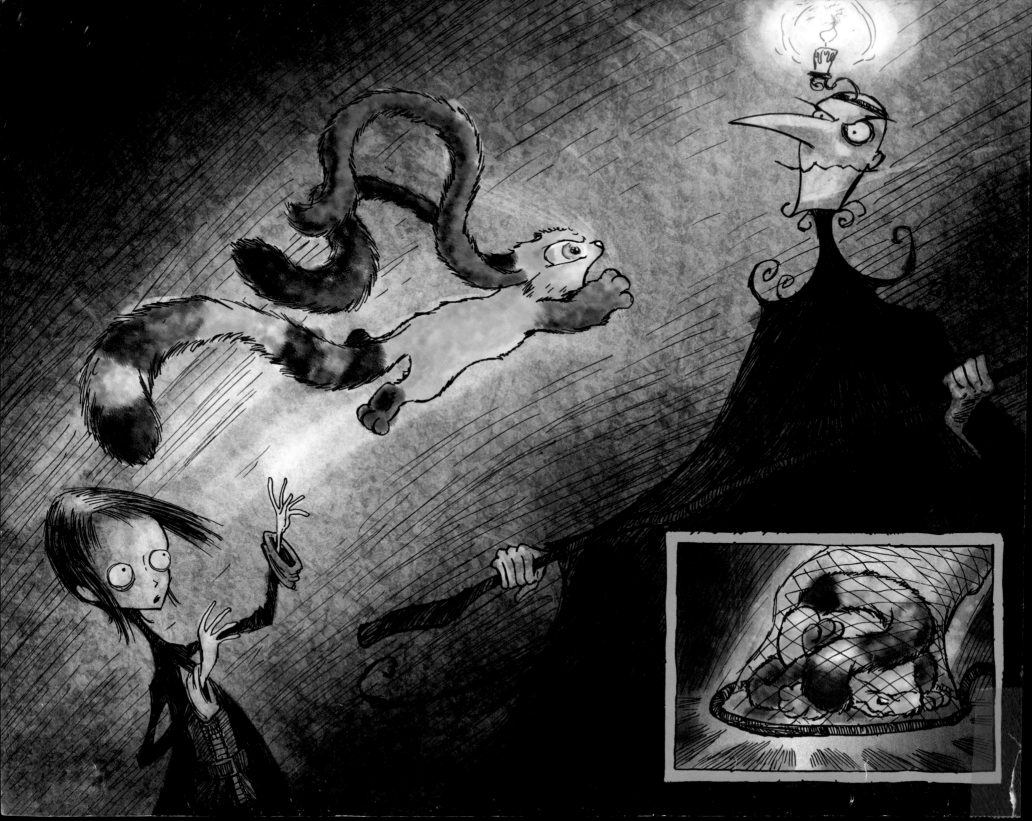

The Prince grabbed the net, causing the color catcher to wobble on the ledge. "If you let go, your fuzzy friend comes with me!"

The Prince released the net.

Viridian and the wooglefoof peered over the ledge.

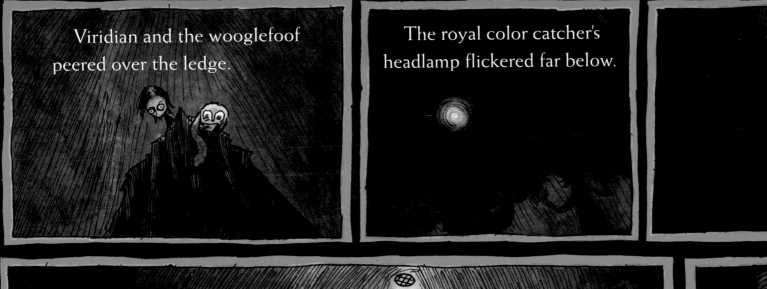

The royal color catcher's headlamp flickered far below.

And color bloomed throughout
the kingdom forever after.